A CHAMPION SPORTS STORY

Tony's Last Touchdown

Benjamin Jarman

Enslow Publishers, Inc.
40 Industrial Road
Box 398
Berkeley Heights, NJ 07922
USA

http://www.enslow.com

This book would not exist without the support of my mother, Judy

Copyright © 2012 by Benjamin Jarman

All rights reserved.

No part of this book may be reproduced by any means
without the written permission of the publisher.

Library of Congress Cataloging-in-Publication Data

Jarman, Benjamin.
    Tony's last touchdown / Benjamin Jarman.
        p. cm. — (A Champion sports story)
    Summary: Although he is the best linebacker in town, Tony must make a difficult
choice between continuing to play football and helping his family when his mother
loses one of her two jobs, his younger brother starts to go astray, and Tony himself
is struggling to pass his math class.
    ISBN 978-0-7660-3885-1
    [1. Football—Fiction. 2. Family problems—Fiction. 3. Poverty—Fiction.
4. Schools—Fiction. 5. African Americans—Fiction.] I. Title.
    PZ7.J2858To 2012
    [Fic]—dc23   2011011888

Paperback ISBN 978-1-4644-0004-9

ePub ISBN 978-1-4645-0452-5

PDF ISBN 978-1-4646-0452-2

Printed in the United States of America

092011 Lake Book Manufacturing, Inc., Melrose Park, IL

10 9 8 7 6 5 4 3 2 1

Cover Illustration: Shutterstock.com.

 # CONTENTS

CHAPTER ONE

Linebacker

The running back smashed through the defensive line and saw Tony out of the corner of his eye. Everyone knew Tony was the best high school linebacker in the city, but the running back sprinted toward the end zone, determined to score a touchdown.

Tony kept his eyes locked on the ball carrier. He watched the running back twist around a tackle, jump over reaching hands, and push away approaching charges. The running back kicked up chunks of turf with each step. To Tony, every move happened in slow motion. He wanted to make sure he could anticipate the runner's moves.

The ball carrier looked forward. He only needed to pass Tony to make it to the end zone. His eyes widened at the sight of the burly linebacker. He didn't recognize him at first, but statistics from the newspaper suddenly flashed in his mind. All the tackles next to Tony's name along with fumble recoveries worried the runner. The great linebacker even had a few touchdowns from fumble recoveries. Tony's physical presence intimidated the runner even more. The linebacker was just over six feet tall and weighed a muscular 220 pounds. However, he moved gracefully and quickly, like a fleet-footed cornerback.

The white lines around the field created a stage for all the athletes, but Tony and the running back were the stars locked in conflict. Tony did not hear the roar of the crowd or his teammates. He did not feel the wind drying the sweat through his helmet. He only saw his opponent surrounded by nothing.

Tony dug his cleats into the turf and squatted as low as he could go. He tightened his muscles just enough to maintain strength but not lose balance. The running back was only a yard away with the football stuffed tightly under his arm.

Dirt mingled with sweat on their faces as the players locked eyes. The running back could not look at Tony anymore; suddenly he knew Tony would tackle him. At this point, he only wanted to avoid humiliation and injury. He had made it past the rest of the defense. That was enough of an accomplishment for him. Tony, on the other hand, was as confident as ever.

Tony pushed forward with both feet. His cheeks shook as his arms and legs powered toward the speedy runner. He did not break eye contact with his opponent.

Tony's hands bashed the bottom of the runner's shoulder pads. He extended his arms, stopping the running back's blind dash. His feet kept charging. The helpless player closed his eyes and began to move in the opposite direction. The force of Tony's blow placed the ball carrier in the air. He was flying backward with Tony in control.

The running back hit the ground on his back with Tony on top. Both players slid across another yard of mud before they came to a stop. Tony never blinked once.

The running back opened his eyes, trembling in the moment. He did not move. He saw Tony's eyes. Their facemasks were the only barriers between them.

Tony looked at his opponent. It could have been the distance between them or the angle of vision, but his opponent's eyes spoke to him. He never thought about their eyes before this play. People were scared of him, but that never stopped him from doing his job. He had seen their eyes during hundreds of previous tackles, but this was the first time he recognized something. He had seen them before—outside the game.

CHAPTER TWO

Student

Sixteen-year-old Tony saw the eyes of his middle-aged math teacher, Ms. Parker. She didn't say anything, but stood straight in her green dress, staring at him. She placed a corrected quiz on his desk, shot a concerned expression in his direction, and continued around the classroom. Tony didn't mind Ms. Parker. It was math that he hated.

Tony didn't want to look at the quiz. He ran his long fingers through his dark hair because he knew the results were poor. He didn't study for the quiz, and he had fallen asleep in class a few times last week. He was already five assignments behind the rest of the class. But math homework was the last thing he wanted to do at night.

He saw Ms. Parker passing a quiz to Shannon, the student in front of him. Tony could see her high score. He and Shannon had gone to the same school since kindergarten. They got along in an easy, relaxed way. Other girls made him nervous because he felt like he had to act like a big shot around them—but not Shannon. She made him comfortable, and he could always make her laugh. They were good friends. Shannon had no problems with math, and Tony knew she would do anything for him. But he was too afraid to ask her for extra study help.

Tony looked down at the failing score on his quiz. He remembered all the guessing involved. Sometimes he didn't even show any work before he answered; he just wrote down anything. Question six made no sense at all. Who cares what percentage of the 238 chickens were laying eggs anyway?

He studied the back of Shannon's head—the small waves of brown hair and the piece of lint on the shoulder of her blue sweater. He needed to

pass this class, and she could make it happen. An "F" meant no football, and football was all that mattered to him. Football made him feel important. It showed everyone who he was, and he was the best football player in school.

He reached his hand out to tap her on the back but stopped inches away. He just couldn't ask her. With a sigh, he sprawled back in his chair and wished class would end so he could get to practice.

CHAPTER THREE

Brother

The Falcons' locker room smelled like dirty socks as the players walked in after practice. An empty Gatorade bottle rolled down the damp floor. The plastic on the bottle echoed across the concrete until the first player arrived, scraping his cleats on the ground.

With a proud grin, Falcons quarterback Craig Danvers slammed his helmet into a rusty locker, looking forward to the game on Friday. His shaved head made him feel confident, and he picked his zits just before he teased a couple teammates. He was pumped about the way practice progressed.

His smile turned into a laugh when he saw Tony enter the room.

"Dude, you rule. High five! I can't get anything by you," Craig said.

"You can when you go wide," Tony responded. "Besides, if you get to me, you got past the front line and those few yards are enough. This game is all about the 10 yards. You got four chances to make it 10 yards. You move 3 or 4 yards a play, and you'll eventually score a touchdown. Lester knows that."

"That little thing? Lucky I get him the ball," Craig said.

Just then, Lester walked into the locker room. He was the shortest guy on the team, and he was the only player who kept his helmet on in the locker room. His long hair fell over his freckled forehead. He looked down as he walked to the other side of the room, avoiding eye contact with his teammates.

"That guy works harder than any of us," Tony said. "And he gets better every week."

Before anyone could respond, Coach Johnson marched out of his office. He always dressed in old tracksuits and cheap sneakers from a discount store. However, he still looked like he could play professional football. His shoulders were wide, and his face was tough.

"That was a pretty good practice, but keep your mind on the game!" Coach shouted. "Don't let your heads get too big."

All the players looked in different directions and continued to their lockers. Soon, Tony heard the trickle of the showers. He was alone, sitting on a bench in the corner of the room. He still carried the extra weight of his shoulder pads. He liked to have a little space after practice. His teammates knew he just needed some time to unwind, so they did not bother him.

He looked at his cleats and noticed the mud caked between the spikes. Playing in the rain was the way to play the game. Football is an outdoor game, and rain only helped. He didn't care if the rain continued through his walk home. He thought about his obligations at home as he started picking at the dirt under his feet. The stream of water from the showers stopped, and the last locker closed. The light in Coach Johnson's office turned off.

"Tony, let's go. You need to get some sleep," Coach said.

The sun was gone before Tony arrived home. The apartment complex that he lived in was not lit very well from the outside. A spider had made a home between the one flickering streetlight and the building wall with its peeling brown paint. Tony didn't need a key to enter the main building.

Once inside, Tony climbed three flights of stairs. The floors were covered with worn red carpet. The gray walls were scraped and scarred by years of furniture moving up and down the hallways. He stepped on an old piece of bubble gum before he reached apartment 379 at the end of the hall.

Tony knocked on the door a few times before someone answered. A smaller version of Tony opened the door with curious eyes. He was nine years old and wore one of Tony's old football jerseys. The remains of a mohawk were etched in his hair.

"What did I tell you about opening the door," Tony asked.

The boy responded, "Don't unlatch the chain."

"Then why did you do it?"

The boy just turned around and walked over to the flickering television in the corner of the dark room. Tony sighed and headed for the tiny kitchen. He opened the refrigerator and found a plastic ice cream container with the soup his mom had made two nights before . . . chicken-vegetable. He dumped what remained into a pan. While it heated on the stove, he found two clean bowls and a box of crackers.

"Tyson! Supper!" Tony yelled.

The smaller boy didn't move.

"Tyson!"

Nothing. Tony walked across the room and clicked off the television.

"Supper. Now!" Tony said.

The nine-year-old slowly moved from the couch to the small table a few feet away.

They ate in silence. Tony had also found a can of pears that they shared for dessert. As they cleaned up the dishes, Tony asked, "You finish your homework?'

"Yes," Tyson responded.

"Show me."

Tyson glanced at his brother with his big brown eyes. Tony shot him that look—his infamous stare. Tyson headed slowly to their small bedroom beside the kitchen, and Tony heard him open a backpack, pull out some books, and flop onto the bed, frustrated by Tony's parenting.

"Mom's rules," said Tony, as he slowly turned to stare at the TV in the corner.

CHAPTER FOUR

Son

Tyson didn't know the man standing by their apartment door, so he watched him without blinking or expression. The man needed a shave and a haircut. His gray jacket had small tears in the back and his jeans were wrinkled. But he had a strong body and half a smile on his face. And he was carrying a television—a nineteen-inch set.

Tony knew him, though. It may have been two years since the last time he stood in that doorway. However, as their eyes met, Tony knew it was his father, Eddie.

"Hey, kid! You're getting pretty big," Eddie said to Tony.

Tony just shrugged his shoulders.

"Don't you have anything to say to your old man? And who's this little ear of corn?"

"I'm not little! And who are you, Mister? What are you doing here by my door?" Tyson said, standing tall.

"Hey, this is my door, too! I'm your dad. I was in the neighborhood and thought maybe you guys could use this new TV."

"Oh, boy! Really? I can't believe it. For me? Awesome! Awesome!" Tyson jumped up and down with excitement.

"Yes, sir! Come on, open this door so we can hook up this baby," Tony's father said.

Tony hesitated but then slowly unlocked the apartment door, and Tyson and his dad hurried into the main room. They moved the coffee table toward the corner of the room and set the TV on top. Then he and Tyson settled onto the couch and started clicking through the channels. Tony stood by the kitchen table.

"Hey, kid, you have any food for your old man?" his father shouted back to him.

Tony reluctantly found an open bag of chips and some bread and meat for sandwiches as he watched his dad charm his little brother.

For the rest of the night, Tyson and his dad watched TV, laughed, and wrestled around on the living room floor. Finally, around 11:00 P.M., Tyson fell asleep on the couch, and Tony carried him into bed, closing the door behind him. Tony tried to sleep, too, but couldn't, knowing that his dad was still there. Early the next morning, he heard the front door open as his mom arrived home from work. He heard their voices—angry at times and frightened, too. It sounded like his dad was demanding money. After about an hour, the front door slammed, and he could hear his mother getting ready for bed, softly crying.

The next morning Tyson was angry. He wanted to know where his dad was and what they had done to him. He was so sure that Tony and his mom had kicked him out. It was many weeks before Tyson did anything other than go to school and stare at the TV.

Tony woke his brother up. Tyson was a deep sleeper and did not wake with a simple call of his name. Tony lightly slapped him in the face to break the sleep. Tony enjoyed this when he was younger, but torturing his brother had grown old.

As Tony got ready for school, he noticed his thighs were sore. He always told himself to stay low when preparing for a tackle. He knew he would have the advantage if he could stay lower than his opponent. All the squatting required to reach that low position strained his muscles, but this was only an afterthought. Tony loved the game, and the pain was only a bonus.

Tony's mother, Jasmine, slept on the couch. She was a small woman with streaks of gray hair, even though she was just in her mid-thirties. The boys rarely said a word in the morning because they knew the importance of her sleep. They also had a routine that required very little speech once mastered.

Their mother stocked shelves at a local grocery store from 9:00 P.M. until 4:00 A.M. Before her night job, she worked as a cook at a nursing home in the neighborhood. The money from these jobs gave her sons enough to survive. When she finally came home very early in the morning, she needed to sleep.

Once the clock radio alarm turned on a Top 40 hit, Tony used the bathroom, found his clothes, and tapped his brother again. His brother used the bathroom while Tony searched the kitchen for anything that could satisfy his appetite. Usually, he found milk or juice and some cereal or bread. Just as he finished stuffing his face, Tyson made his way to the kitchen. Tony passed his brother a bowl of cereal and inspected his outfit.

"Fix your collar," Tony whispered.

"What?" Tyson responded.

"You heard me. Come on. Eat your breakfast. We gotta go."

Once outside, Tony pushed past a couple of teens in hooded sweatshirts sitting on the front steps of his apartment and stood impatiently on the sidewalk. Tyson exited the building and paused on the steps by the boys.

"Hey, little man," said one of the teens.

"What's up?" Tyson said.

"Let's go, man," Tony yelled. "I don't want to be late."

"Later, guys," Tyson said.

Tyson caught up to Tony. They did not say anything until they reached the block with Tyson's school.

"Make sure you get home right after school," Tony said. "We gotta help mom as much as possible."

"Why you gotta be on me all the time?" Tyson complained. "Don't I do the same thing every day like I'm supposed to?"

"I was your age, too. I remember how hard it was to follow the rules," Tony said. "Now make sure you get your homework and get home when the bell rings. See you later."

Eventually, Tony jumped the fence bordering the high school and saw Shannon walk off the bus. Their eyes met. She was shorter than Tony and didn't wear makeup because she didn't need it. She wore a Falcons letter jacket with volleyball honors, skinny jeans, and boots. Tony jogged over, and they walked toward the building together.

"Did you finish your math work?" Shannon asked.

"No," Tony said.

"No? You're kidding me, right?"

"Listen, Shannon, I get home late from practice. I have to fix supper for Tyson and help him with his homework. I'm just too beat to do Parker's work, too," Tony sighed.

"You poor boy—what a tough life for our football superstar. But math isn't going to disappear because you're tired. What are you going to do?" she asked.

"I don't know. We've got a big game on Friday. If I can just get through this week, then maybe I can concentrate more next week. Help me out, Shannon. What can I do?" Tony asked.

Shannon stopped. She stood quietly on the first step leading into the building, studying Tony's face. She stared into his eyes like she might find her answer there. Then she reached into her backpack and pulled out a worn green notebook.

"Today's assignment is in the back," she said.

"Aww, Shannon, you're the best. I'll get this back to you before class."

"You'll do more than that! You have to meet with me to go over the assignment. It won't do you any good to just copy my paper. You need to understand what you're doing so you are ready for the next test. I will see you after school, right?" Shannon asked with authority.

"Right! Thanks, Shannon. I really mean it," Tony said.

CHAPTER FIVE

Boot Camp

Football warm-ups were especially difficult after school because of the humidity. Dew on the torn grass left a sweet smell in the air. The Falcons players said little, knowing the way practices always started.

Coach Johnson and his assistants walked around the field arranging abandoned tires. A few others were placing pads on the sled, a movable and padded post used to practice contact. Coach tossed one more tire on the ground and put his whistle against his lips.

The sound of the coach's whistle signaled the start of practice. Most of the players, excluding

Tony and Lester, dreaded that sound because it meant the beginning of warm-ups. Yet everyone sprinted to the coach, even though they may have lacked the motivation.

"You know the drill," Coach Johnson yelled. "Line up for boot camp!"

A quarter of the team formed a group in front of the sled. A few slightly smaller groups moved toward the rope steppers and the powerblast. Craig Danvers took other players to a set of tackling dummies resting on the ground by the chutes. Tony and Lester were the only players to move to the tires—the most difficult drill—because they loved the physical challenge.

"Let's go!" Coach Johnson shouted. "I need a few of you at the sled to move to the tires."

Terry grunted and followed Coach Johnson's command. Jesse, Joe, Matt, and Pat lowered their heads and hustled over to the tires, too. Most of the team hated this station even before they touched the first tire.

"You gotta do it sometime, right?" Tony said.

"Okay, get those helmets on," Coach Johnson said. "You're not gonna be on the field without a helmet, so you cannot practice without one."

The team could hear the cheerleaders practicing on the other side of the school and the last school bus leaving the grounds. Now even those sounds were muffled as players snapped on their helmets. Craig was the last to put on the protective covering.

"Okay, I have my watch out," Coach Johnson said. "Five minutes at each station. No stopping! You have fifteen seconds to rotate to the next station with the rest of your group. Let's do this!"

The coach blew his whistle, and the team jumped into action at each station. Tony lowered himself on all fours and started navigating his way through the tires. To survive this station, each player needed to crawl across a series of old tires. The player's legs became increasingly difficult to lift in the required position. Tony made his way across the tires in no time. Lester followed, and, though he did not enjoy the station, he was fast and finished on Tony's tail.

When a player made it to the end of the station, he had to run to the back of the line. The cycle continued for five minutes, and the assistant coach at the station did not let anyone rest. On Tony's third time through, the player in front of him fell on his face. Tony said nothing, brought his clumsy teammate Matt to his feet, and moved forward. On the fifth round, Coach Johnson blew his whistle, and the groups rotated as each coach clapped his encouragement.

The next station Tony's group approached required pure forward power. The powerblast was a gate closed by spring-powered pads. Players could not move the pads with their arms alone. Players had to run at full speed and smash through the gate. This station was the most fun, so when Coach Johnson blew his whistle, Tony made the springs vibrate.

When the five minutes expired, and the coach blew his whistle for the next rotation, Tony's group moved to the sled. Seven tackling dummies were attached to a sled. Each member of the group lined up across from a dummy, crouched down, and attacked the dummy. Each player used a shoulder to lean on the sled. They moved across the field if the dummies were hit hard enough.

To make this station even more challenging, the heaviest assistant coach yelled at the group while riding the sled. Tony's group took its first shot at the sled and failed to make it move. They all hit the dummies, but they were losing power after ten minutes in the physically draining practice.

"Come on!" yelled the heavy coach. "Reset. You can do this."

"Get mad, guys," said Tony, as he thought about his math homework. "Think of your worst enemy, and see that enemy in the dummy."

The group reset and launched at the dummies on the heavy coach's command. Pat, Jesse, and Matt yelled this time and managed to lift the sled off the ground for a second. The coach looked slightly concerned as he tightened his grip on the iron machine. Once the sled settled, the players continued to push with their legs. They chopped with their feet and made the sled move across the field. Some of the players were still yelling as their legs burned with the strain of the drill. The team hated the tires the most, but this station wasn't far behind. Joe, a tight end in Tony's group, fell over, but the sled kept moving behind the force of the players. Matt fell, and the sled almost stopped. Sweat dripped into Tony's eyes, stinging them, but the coach's whistle sounded, and the five minutes at that station were up.

Tony's group hustled to the next station and lined up at the rope steppers. The steppers were a series of ropes suspended a foot above the ground. With the shrill sound of the whistle, Tony's group jumped between each rope without tripping.

The team didn't mind this station because players could stand upright—squatting strained those underdeveloped muscles. As Tony's group continued through the station, Matt became tangled in the ropes and tripped. The assistant coach at this station knew it wasn't as hard as the other stations, so he yelled loudly—and a lot. By this time, though, most players had motivation to move forward because they knew they had only one station left.

Tackling dummies rested at the last station— the chutes. With the chutes, players found partners within the group. One player grabbed a dummy and moved to the back of the chutes. The other crouched down at the front of the chutes, charged forward at the assistant coach's command, and tried to make it past the player with the dummy. The series of metal pipes that form the chute forced the player to stay low. If the clang of metal was heard, it was from the chutes. Craig could only man a dummy at this station, because he had to protect his throwing arm.

Because this was the last station, many players could not stay low enough to avoid the metal pipes. Their legs hurt, and they could not reach the depth required for the drill. Tony partnered with Terry, an offensive guard. They were about the same size, and they met on the practice field often. Both players enjoyed holding the dummy, but only Tony could make it through the chute and past the dummy. At one point, Tony used the dummy to knock Terry back into the chutes.

When Coach Johnson blew his whistle to signal the end of boot camp, many players took off their helmets and fell over exhausted. Others ran to get water. Tony simply put his hands on his head and walked it off. He knew his lungs would receive the most air standing in this position.

Eventually, all the players took a knee around Coach Johnson.

"We do that every day for a reason. Remember this in the fourth quarter when your muscles start burning. We have a game on Friday against the top-ranked team in the conference. When we're at practice, stay focused and think about the game. Concentrate and forget about everything else. Now we only have two days left to practice so let's make it count. Circle up on the field so we can stretch and scrimmage. Huddle it up here. Craig, let's go!"

The whole team gathered around Craig and put their hands in the air.

"On three, we say 'Go team,'" Craig said. "One, two, three!"

The whole team filled the air with Craig's command and jogged to the main field.

After practice, Tony exited the locker room and saw Shannon sitting on the floor.

"Dang!" Tony said. "I forgot! I'm sorry, I'm sorry, I'm sorry! We were supposed to meet after school, right? I really messed up, didn't I?"

"Yes, you did. I stuck my neck out to help you. I gave you my assignment, which could get me in a lot of trouble, and you can't even meet me after school for a few minutes to go over the work. What's the matter with you? You're using our friendship to get out of your responsibilities." Shannon angrily stared at him until he finally had to look away. She was right.

"I messed up," Tony said. "My mind has been on so many things lately. My brother, my mom, the team, my dad."

"Well, somewhere in those list of things you're thinking about, you had better add math. Simply copying my work won't do you any good at quiz time. You'll still fail. You have to let me explain the work to you. It's not that hard if you'd pay attention in class and spend fifteen minutes or so with me each afternoon. You're doing well in all your other classes. If you can make time for football, you can make time for math."

Tony felt awful. What could he say? She was right. Before he had a chance to apologize again, Shannon handed him her notebook and said, "Tomorrow's assignment is in the back. I have to

get home for supper now. We will try this again tomorrow afternoon. Don't let me down, because this is your last chance." She picked up her things and hurried down the hallway.

Tony watched her hair wave as she turned the corner and then looked at the numbers on the last page of the notebook. They made no sense. The last time math had made sense to him was many years ago, when his dad had helped him.

CHAPTER SIX

Math Tutor

Tony sat at the table across from his father. In fourth grade, Tony and his father worked on math every night after supper. Tyson was just a toddler, already asleep in his bed. His mother would not be home from her job at the hospital for another hour. It was just Tony and his dad. His dad was really good at math and had shown Tony how to use a multiplication table. His grades were improving, and he even found he liked math class most of the time. But what he really liked was spending time with his dad.

"What am I really gonna need to use this for?" Tony asked.

"When you don't have a job, and you are counting the pennies, math is all you've got," his dad said. "Some days the most important job is knowing that four dollars can get you eight cans of soup down at the Red Owl. And milk and bananas are always cheaper at the PDQ. Or how about when you have to ride the bus? Is it cheaper to pay your fare every day or to buy a pass for the month?"

"I'm gonna have a big, fast car when I'm older so I won't ever ride the bus," bragged nine-year-old Tony.

His dad laughed. "Well, squirt, good for you. And I hope you'll take your old man for a ride in that big, fast car. But sometimes things happen, and you don't have a job. Then forget about the car or even enough money for the bus. Forget about everything."

Tony looked into his dad's eyes. There was sadness but also anger. He was suddenly afraid that their math time at the table was over—that his dad had lost interest and would leave to go out with his friends, as he often did at night.

"Hey, Dad, what about problem twelve? I just don't understand if I should multiply or divide."

A few seconds passed, and his dad picked up the pencil again.

Tony could not keep his eyes open in math class. Yesterday's boot camp practice had been long and difficult, but that night he couldn't sleep. He and Tyson had a long battle about homework after supper. He had more and more trouble getting Tyson to listen, especially after football practice, when all he wanted to do was eat and go to sleep. And then there was the problem with Shannon. He needed to get his act together in math class and stop relying on her brains to carry him through it.

"Anthony! I hope we're not disturbing your nap back there." His eyes popped open. It was Ms. Parker, standing in the front of the room with one hand on her hip and the other holding a piece of chalk. She looked like she was deciding whether to throw it at him or not.

"Sorry, Ms. Parker," Tony replied quietly.

He sat up straighter and stared at the board, but he really wasn't getting it. Finally, the bell rang. Rather than hurrying out with the others, Tony slowly gathered his books and papers. When everyone else had left the room, he went up to the teacher's desk.

"I am very sorry, Ms. Parker," Tony said. "I am falling behind in this class. Is there any way I could do some work to get extra credit? I've just been so busy with football and other stuff."

"Except for the last two days, you haven't been handing in your regular work. What makes you think you can do extra assignments if you can't even do the daily work?" Ms. Parker said, staring at him.

"I will try. I know I have to do better."

Ms. Parker shook her head. "I don't give extra credit, and, even if I did, it wouldn't help you. You had Fs on the last three quizzes. I can't give you a passing grade if you don't know the math."

Now Tony shook his head. What was he going to do? There was nothing he could say to her. Ms. Parker continued. "This Friday's quiz is very important. If you don't pass it, I have no choice but to tell Coach Johnson about your grades. You know the rules. You can't play with failing grades."

Tony's mind was swirling.

"Let me finish," Ms. Parker said. "If you *do* pass it, you will have some breathing room. It will pull your grade up enough to keep you going until the end-of-the-quarter exam later this month. And you did do very well on these last two homework assignments, which will help you on the Friday quiz. It isn't hopeless."

Tony knew it was hopeless. But he couldn't tell Ms. Parker that he did so well on the homework only because he copied Shannon's. How could he pass this quiz? And what about the team? Who would he be without football? Now everyone knew him. He was the best linebacker in the city. Football was everything.

He nodded his head at Ms. Parker, mumbled good-bye, and headed out the door to the locker room to get ready for practice.

At practice, Tony put his hand in the middle of the Falcons defensive huddle. This was the fourteenth play of the scrimmage, and every player wanted to make good use of the time.

The other defensive players placed a hand over Tony's hand. As the best player on the team, the Falcons defense looked to Tony as their leader.

Tony yelled, "One, two, three!" followed by, "Break!" in unison with the team.

Each defensive player ran to a position. The front line assembled on the 50-yard line. Tony moved to a ready position and looked at Travis, another linebacker. Travis looked pumped up and a little crazy as he waited for the snap of the football. He nodded to Tony.

The offense came out of its huddle and approached the line of scrimmage. Craig, the quarterback, surveyed the defense as he crouched behind the center. The center palmed the ball and snorted at his defensive opponent.

Craig yelled, "Down, set." He looked down the line and back toward the goal again while Lester ran a pattern behind him. "Hut!"

The helmets and shoulder pads of the offensive and defensive lines collided like a car crash in rush hour. The defensive line strained to sack the quarterback. One defensive tackle brought himself lower than his offensive opponent, but he could not overpower him. The tackle roared as he fell hard to the ground.

Meanwhile, Craig searched for a receiver. Fifteen yards ahead, two of his receivers were covered by the defense. He saw his third receiver 10 yards in front of him, running from one sideline to the other. Craig pulled the ball behind his head and launched his arm forward like a catapult. The ball spiraled toward the open receiver.

The receiver focused on the ball as it sailed toward his ready hands. He stopped moving for a second to connect with the path of the ball. The ball touched his fingertips and settled into his palms as he began to turn toward the end zone.

Suddenly, the crunch of Tony's shoulder pads hitting the receiver echoed in all the players' ears. Tony wrapped his arms around the receiver and took him straight to the ground. The receiver managed to retain the ball as he went to the ground, but he was never able to fully turn to see the goal.

The coaches clapped for both sides. They were proud of the pass and catch and the yards gained, and equally happy about the immediate tackle.

This was just a practice, and both sides needed to focus on their strengths and improve on their weaknesses. Nevertheless, this play looked very good to everyone on the field.

Coach Johnson blew his whistle and sent in another play to the offense. Both sides formed a huddle and listened to the captains and coaches discuss the next play. Both sides broke huddle at the same time and lined up at the ball. Just before Craig received the ball from center, he smiled at Tony, who stared back at the quarterback.

The chaos after the snap was settling as the offensive linemen maneuvered their opponents with each block. They managed to create a hole between the left guard and left tackle just as Craig handed the ball to Lester. Lester moved for the hole and squeezed through because of his small size and quickness.

Once past the front line, Lester faced Travis, who charged right at him. Just before they made contact, Lester twisted around Travis. Travis's middle finger touched Lester's jersey, but he was not fast enough to tackle him. After that, Lester saw no players between him and the end zone.

The defensive line had turned toward Lester by this point. Tony began the play by following a receiver, but he had spotted Lester as he moved toward Travis. Tony now focused his attention on Lester. A defensive back was able to slow Lester's forward drive just enough to give Tony time to catch up. Lester was shuffling by the defensive back as Tony slammed into him from behind to end the play.

Tony pulled Lester off the scarred turf.

"You okay, man?" Tony asked.

Lester nodded his head.

"He's ready for more!" Craig yelled.

"Let's go. Next play!" called a coach.

The players discussed the plan in their huddles and prepared for the next play. Each player on offense and defense looked determined to outplay the other side, even though they were all part of the same team.

Sweat drenched the players' uniforms, and their legs jiggled with tension to prepare for the real, top-ranked opponent. They knew each side was simply conditioning the other for the big game on Friday.

Craig took his offense to the line with the ball. The defense was ready. The center looked ahead and snapped the ball on Craig's signal.

Both sides collided, and Craig stepped back for a pass. Both Tony and Travis blitzed, attempting to tackle the quarterback behind the line of scrimmage. Tony met the opposition and pushed the offensive blocks into the backfield. Travis roared through a lone offensive guard and set his sights on the quarterback.

Craig saw the pass rush and ran toward the sideline, away from the clump of savagery around the line of scrimmage. Travis raced after him as he tossed the ball to the sidelines. Travis saw the ball disappear from Craig's hand but tackled him nonetheless.

"What are you doing?" Coach Johnson yelled. "You saw him toss the ball!"

"Get off me, man!" Craig shouted.

Travis said nothing and ran back to his defensive teammates.

"One more move like that and I'm pulling you," Coach Johnson said. "No huddle this time. Just line up in your positions on the 50-yard line."

Coach dragged Craig and Lester to the sideline and discussed the play. Everyone took a knee in their positions and watched in anticipation.

Tony looked at Travis.

"You alright, man?" Tony asked.

"I just let Lester get by me and it got me hyped," Travis said. "Craig ticks me off, too."

"Just cool it," Tony said.

Craig and Lester left the coach and returned to their positions.

"I'm just gonna tell you we are running a tackle trap on the right," an assistant coach said to Tony. "I want to see how you adjust when I tell you the play. Run it."

"Tackle trap!" Tony yelled.

"Tackle trap!" Travis yelled.

"Down, set, hut!" Craig shouted.

Craig took the ball from the center and turned to hand it off to Lester. The defensive line had little time to react, and the offensive line created the tackle trap. A hole in the line formed just as Lester received the handoff, and he drove the ball through the opening.

Lester faced Tony and no one else before the end zone. Their eyes locked. Tony knew he had to be careful with Lester's quickness. He also had to get very low to match Lester's size. They'd met hundreds of times in the past, under the same circumstances, and Lester knew he could not beat Tony. Regardless, Lester did not blink as he charged at Tony full speed.

The players connected with a clean hit, and Tony, as usual, pushed Lester on his back. Lester performed no special moves, and he did not slow down. He took the hit, gained 5 yards for the offense, and the coaches clapped in approval.

"That's a hit," Coach Johnson said. "Let's take it in."

Lester jumped to his feet and ran to the locker room. He tossed the ball behind him. The ball hit the ground and rolled to a stop against Tony's kneepad. He still sat on the ground from the last play. He was not injured, and he was not relaxing. He was, however, shocked from the blow he had received from the little running back. Was Lester getting that much better or was Tony slowing down? Maybe his thoughts were on his problems off the field. He thought of Lester, his grades, and his family.

After practice, Tony found Shannon at the back of the library with some open books. He kept his promise to meet her today after practice, and he could tell from her smile that she was very happy to see him.

"Okay, let's go back a few lessons to review. You need to understand the work on pages eighty-nine and ninety before we can look at this week's work," Shannon said.

"Boy, you don't give a guy a chance to catch his breath! You make Ms. Parker look like a quiet little mouse," Tony joked.

Shannon laughed. "Well, hot shot, if you are going to play in the game on Friday, we have our work cut out for us. Let's get going."

For the next forty-five minutes, Shannon reviewed each part of the chapter. She made him work every problem until he could show her that he could do them correctly without her help. At times, he wanted to push the math book off the table and stomp out of the library. At other times, he could see that Shannon seemed ready to lose her temper and patience, too. But they stuck with it. She walked him through each page, step-by-step, and did not move on until Tony could explain every word. In the end, she gave him a quiz she had made up of problems that would probably be on Ms. Parker's quiz. He nervously watched as Shannon corrected his paper.

"Congratulations! Only two wrong. You will pass this quiz with no trouble," she boasted.

Tony jumped out of his chair. He grabbed Shannon's hands and danced around the table shouting, "I am the greatest!" until the librarian came over and told them to sit down and be quiet.

Shannon giggled as she began to gather her books and papers. "You are one crazy linebacker. But I knew you could do this if you just gave it your undivided attention. I know football is important to you, but the future . . . well, school has to fit in somewhere, too."

"I know. It's just easier and more fun to tackle someone." They both laughed. "Sometimes I have so much rolling around in my head that there is no room for school. So if you see me slip up, just smack me on the back of my head."

"I'm happy to help . . . anytime," Shannon said.

"Thanks, Shannon." Their eyes met for a minute. "Speaking of homework, I've gotta get home and help my brother. I'm late already."

They grabbed their backpacks and headed out the door.

CHAPTER SEVEN

Lost

Tony opened the door to his apartment and noticed that the television was not turned on. He tossed his backpack on the ground and walked to the refrigerator. There was enough milk in the jug for half a glass. He pulled out a glass with a Michigan State logo on the side and emptied the container.

"Where are you?" Tony yelled.

Nobody answered. Tony looked around. He thought about *Madden 2012*, a game his brother played religiously. He could imagine the graphics on the powerless television.

"Tyson, where are you?"

Tony placed his glass on a table and walked down the hall to the room he shared with his brother. The door was closed. He thought he would scare his brother, so instead of knocking on the door, he smashed his way into the room.

"What are you doing?" shouted Tony, as he barged into the room.

The blankets on the beds were still unmade. Toys and clothes cluttered the floor. The window was closed. No sound greeted him. The room was silent.

An unsettling feeling gripped Tony. His brother was supposed to be home. His mother worked until early morning. Tony knew he was responsible for his little brother. He had felt this way one other time when he had lost Tyson at the toy store.

His brother needed to come home right after school and lock the door. Tony had schoolwork and a football game on his mind, but this was much more important.

Tony turned around in his room and ran into the hall. He left the apartment without locking the door and ran down the three flights of stairs leading to the street.

The last streaks of sunlight disappeared, and darkness overpowered the streetlights. Five lights per block were not enough. He continued sprinting down the street like it was the second boot camp of the day. He crushed the fall leaves under his feet as he ran. He saw a neighbor returning from the grocery store.

"Hey, have you seen my little brother out here?" Tony asked.

"I haven't seen a thing out here," replied the neighbor. "Way too dark, man."

"If you see him, tell him to get home right away," Tony said.

Tony did not listen to the neighbor's reply. He continued running down the street. He knew kids liked to hang out near the grocery store, so he ran to check for him there. As he ran across the street, a car braked quickly to avoid Tony, and the driver honked his horn. Tony just kept going.

As he approached the grocery store parking lot, he saw a group of teens from his neighborhood in a huddle. He barely recognized the kids in the shadows, and he did not know them by name. They were older than he was and seemed to be laughing about something. Suddenly, he noticed his brother in the middle of the huddle.

"Back off," yelled Tony, pushing his way toward Tyson. "Get out of the way."

Tyson saw his brother and stopped smiling. He knew he was in trouble. Tony pulled him away from the group of older teens.

"Just hanging with the little man," one of the guys joked.

"Shut up!" Tony yelled.

"Be cool. We were there for him, man," said another.

"It's okay, Tony," Tyson said, looking at Tony. "We were just hanging."

"I don't want to hear it," Tony said. "You can't do this. Let's go."

Tyson looked back at the boys while they snickered in the darkness. Tony held Tyson's hand as they walked back to the apartment.

CHAPTER EIGHT

Man of the House

Tony sat in a chair reading a comic book, while his mom waited for their clothes to finish drying. His mother stared out the front window, eyes drooping, exhausted from working two jobs. Suddenly, she stood up and ran out the door of the laundromat, holding Tyson in her arms, and crossed the street to where Tony's father stood. During her dash across the street, Tyson lost a shoe and started crying.

"Are you kidding me?" yelled Jasmine when she reached the other sidewalk.

Eddie saw his wife and the anger in her face and turned away from her, stunned. He kept walking away from her, trying to ignore her words.

"Where are you going?" Jasmine continued. "We haven't seen you in eight months! I can't do this alone. You need to stop right now!"

Eddie continued walking away from his wife at an increased pace.

"Stop! Look at your son!" yelled Jasmine as she followed her husband down the sidewalk. "Are you gonna walk away from him? Tyson and Anthony need a father. I can't do this alone!"

Jasmine continued following Eddie down the street, yelling at him, with Tyson crying on her shoulder. The words became too soft for Tony to hear as he watched his family disappear from the laundromat window.

Tony's mother was awake when Tony came into the kitchen for breakfast. Wrapped up in her robe, she slowly sipped from her cup of coffee. She made eye contact with her son.

"How have you been doing?" she asked.

"Fine, mom," Tony replied.

Tony scrambled around the kitchen to find breakfast. He settled for a piece of bread and some strawberry jelly. He pulled out his math book to look over the last few problems that he did not finish yesterday.

"Tyson, get up!" he yelled.

"Can I talk to you for a minute, son?" his mother asked, without moving.

"What's up, mom?" he responded.

"I need you to sit over here," she said.

Tony shut his eyes for a second, closed his math book, and sat in a chair in front of his mom. She seriously, but lovingly, looked at him for a moment. He smiled back, hoping he wasn't in trouble for the previous night.

"What's up?" he asked.

"Can't I just look at my son for a moment?" she responded. "I love you. You are the greatest thing in my life. I can't believe the things my son can do. You make me so proud."

Startled, Tony asked, "What's the matter?"

"Son, I know you work hard, and I know we are struggling to make it," she said. "You are the man this family needs, and you can make it better for us. But, son, I lost my job. I need you to help us out and get a job of your own."

Tony was shocked and stopped listening to his mother. One thing after another flashed in his head: math, Shannon, Tyson, the game on Friday, and now, his mother. It all hit him with such force that he lost his breath for a minute.

"Anthony, I know this is hard for you," his mom said. "But I know we can count on you. It's only temporary. I'm up now so I can start looking for a new job. But until I find one, I need your help to pay the rent. You understand me, Anthony?"

Tony could not respond. He looked at his hands. He saw his father. He did not know where his father was or what he would do, but he knew he didn't want to be like his father. He wanted to support his family, and he knew he could learn from his father's mistakes.

His mom tilted her head and said, "Anthony?"

Tony snapped out of it and looked his mom in the eye. He knew that he needed to support his family.

"I understand, mom," he said. "I will look for a job. We can do this. We always do."

CHAPTER NINE

Responsibilities

At practice, Coach Johnson was particularly hard on the team because of tomorrow's game. Near the end of practice, the scrimmage began to take a toll on Tony. Lester had received the ball more often than usual and had collided with Tony several times. The sun began to disappear in the autumn afternoon as Coach Johnson sent a play to the offensive huddle.

"You ready, Tony?" Travis said. "Coach hasn't tried the tackle trap yet, and you know he loves to practice that play."

Tony gave Travis a questioning look.

"Do I look like I'm not ready?" Tony replied, curiously.

The day was not as hot as it had been earlier in the week, but work on and off the field had taken a toll on Tony's mind. He wasn't tired on the field; he was never tired there. But he wasn't excited either. More than anything, Tony was concerned.

Craig broke the huddle and approached the ball with his offensive line. He wiped the sweat out of his eyes. He placed his hands between the legs of his center, ready for the snap. Both the offensive and defensive lines moved to a ready position, one hand and two feet on the ground.

"Ready, set, hike!" Craig yelled.

Craig immediately turned and handed the ball to Lester. The large offensive linemen moved surprisingly quickly to open a hole for Lester. The defensive line could not keep up.

Lester and Tony met again, and they did not change their behavior. They charged at one another with little thought for the aftermath of the play. Both players were ready for impact. They ran at each other with no fear.

When Lester and Tony collided, Tony tackled Lester as usual. The difference this time around came through sheer force. Tony usually pushed

Lester backward. This time, though, Lester was so determined that he knocked Tony backward. Lester went down with a gain of 6 yards instead of the usual five. Tony laid on his back.

After practice, Tony walked home, completely worn out. He and his brother ate dinner silently, then Tony went straight to bed.

The night before the big game, he dreamed of playing catch with his father. They were in a huge field of green grass surrounded by forest on all sides. The sun was high in the sky, and birds looked for shelter under white clouds.

"Make sure you follow through on your pass, my man," Tony's father said.

"I know dad, but I'm not a quarterback," Tony said.

Tony threw the ball to his father. His father had to lunge to catch the ball. As he got to his feet and turned to face his son again, Tony's father was not smiling. He took a hard look at Tony and roared.

Suddenly, Tony's father started charging at him. Tony wrestled with his father often while growing up, but it was always for fun. This time, his dad did not look like he was playing around. Tony moved as low as possible, ready for the collision. His father had a mean look on his face, as the distance between the two grew smaller. Everything disappeared except his father. Even the roaring sound coming from his father's open mouth went quiet.

As they connected, Tony woke up. He looked at the clock. He was late for class.

At school, Shannon sat in the hall with Tony, going over a few problems before the quiz.

"You are pretty quiet this morning. Worried about the test or the game?" Shannon asked.

"Both, I guess . . . and more," Tony said. He stopped. Should he tell her more? Should he tell her about being late and finding Tyson hanging out at the grocery store with the older boys? Should he tell her about his mom losing her job, or about how money for his family was suddenly becoming more important than math problems, football games, or anything else? *No.* One problem at a time.

"I am still having trouble with these decimal points. Could you explain it one more time?"

Shannon opened her textbook, got out a clean piece of paper, and started working sample problems for Tony. After a few, he took the pencil from her hand and worked a few on his own. While moving a decimal into the correct position, Tony felt Shannon's lips on his cheek. For a moment they both looked at each other shyly. Then they burst out laughing.

"I just know you will do great on this quiz," Shannon said.

"I feel good about it, too. Okay, Ms. Parker, bring on that quiz. I'm in my three-point stance, ready to rip apart those problems. Let's go!"

They picked up their books and headed down the hall to Ms. Parker's room. One problem at a time, Tony thought. Math first . . . then football . . . then family.

CHAPTER TEN

Late for the Big Game

The only light came from the end of the locker room tunnel. Each player looked like an armored ogre emerging from a cave for battle. Craig led the Falcons onto the field, and the fans roared from the bleachers above. The players maintained their energy by running a lap around the field.

The sun was gone, but nobody noticed with the bright flare of the field lights. The Falcons' top-ranked opponent, the Spartans, already stood on the field in warm-up formation.

Their uniforms were dark blue and even the kicker seemed larger than the average teenager. Each player looked like a chess piece listening to the instructions of the captain. They stretched and performed squats, barking numbers in unison for each repetition.

As Craig led his players to their side of the field, Tony ran out of the locker room—late. He quickly snapped his chinstrap and smacked the top of his helmet to make sure it was ready. The crowd recognized the number and cheered in support. They knew the game was a sure win with Tony on the field.

Even with all the support, Tony knew he was falling behind. He was late to the game because he was late to school. He was late to school because he needed to make sure his brother was safe. One responsibility was leading to another. He blinked and focused his stress into a passion he could use on the field.

"Come on, man," yelled Craig just as he began stretching the team.

As co-captain with Craig, Tony led the warm-ups with his quarterback. The whole team was pumped to see Tony. No player faltered during sit-ups or push-ups. The roar of each repetition from the opposing team was now met with an equally intimidating call from Tony and his teammates.

As warm-ups finished, Craig signaled his offense into a quick huddle, and Tony called for his defense. Tony tried to keep his mind on the game. Each member of the starting defense looked at him for instructions.

"Everyone needs to have his mind on the game!" Tony shouted. "Those guys look big and they can bark, but can they play?"

"No!" shouted the defense in unison.

"What?" Tony asked.

"No!" replied the defense with even more passion.

Just before Tony broke the huddle to practice a few plays, the referee blew his whistle, calling for the captains to meet in the center of the field. It was time for the coin toss.

Tony and Craig ran to the middle of the field and were met by two large players from the opposing side. The Spartans captains never took off their helmets and remained in the shadows of their face masks.

"The Falcons are the home team so the Spartans get to make the call for the coin toss," said the ref.

The referee showed the coin to both sides and tossed it in the air.

"Tails!" yelled a masked Spartan.

The coin landed on tails.

"How do you want to start?" asked the ref to the Spartans.

"The ball," responded one of the faceless Spartans.

Tony and Craig returned to Coach Johnson

"You okay, man?" Craig asked.

"The team will be okay," responded Tony without looking at Craig.

Craig continued to look at Tony's blank face, but he knew he had to get Tony's head back in the game.

"I'm gonna get that ball into their end zone; you keep it out of our end zone," Craig said. "Make it happen."

"Sure, man," Tony said.

"Look," Craig said. "You got us on the field late. You don't say anything, and you look scared!

I tell you now, we are not going to win if you don't have your head in the game!"

Tony ignored Craig. He sprinted ahead to his defense, knowing he had to get them ready for the field first.

Special teams prepared for kickoff when Coach Johnson grabbed Tony's shoulder pads.

"You know I have to bench you because you were late," Coach Johnson said. "What's going on? Anything you want to tell me?"

"I'm okay, coach, seriously," Tony said. "I'm really sorry. It hasn't happened before, and it won't happen again."

The coach looked Tony in the eye and then back at the field as special teams prepared for the start of the game. The ref blew his whistle, and both sides went to a ready position.

Frank Bellow, the kicker, stepped to the ball for the Falcons and kicked it to a Spartans kick returner on the 15-yard line. The returner did not perform any special moves, and he did not veer toward the sideline. Instead, he ran straight toward the Falcons kickoff team. The returner met his first opponent and hit him hard enough that he would not play for the rest of the game. The kick returner was down at the Spartans 33-yard line when three Falcons tackled him. The Spartans had gained 18 yards on the return.

Joseph Carey was Tony's replacement. Tony knew the rules: You can't start if you are late. He was never late, but he had no choice in the matter. Besides, Tony had trained Joseph. He knew the defense would manage without him until Coach put Tony back in the game at the beginning of the second quarter.

The Spartans' first play was a run. The Spartans were a rushing team. Falcons players could tell by the wall that formed from their offensive line. The Spartans running backs had little problem moving the ball and the clock because of the huge offensive line and the coach's game plan.

Though the mess of linemen looked chaotic, the sheer size of the offensive line was enough to create holes for the Spartans runners. Four or five yards per play kept the ball moving and wore out the Falcons defense. Eight and a half minutes were used up to move the ball from the Spartans 33-yard line to the Falcons 7-yard line.

Furious, Tony spoke from the sideline for the first time during the game. "Remember boot camp. Don't let them wear you out!"

Tony's words were useless. After so many rushing plays, the Spartans wide receiver ran a route into the end zone. The Falcons defense had focused so much attention on stopping the run that they did not see the quarterback's play fake. They were not ready for the pass. The receiver was in the end zone—wide open. The Spartans took a 7–0 lead with a little more than two minutes left in the first quarter.

The Falcons ran the Spartans' kickoff to the 19-yard line, and Craig brought his offense onto the field. The Spartans offensive line also played on the defensive line. They did not seem bothered by the lengthy run during the first half of the quarter. Sweat combined with the dirt on their faces, making them look like the living dead. Craig's offense couldn't even see them breathing.

Craig called for the snap and didn't notice two defensive tackles approaching. They tackled him in no time.

Back in the huddle, Craig yelled, "Where is my blocking? I can't even hand the ball off. Get it together line. These guys don't look tired, but they are. You fight Tony every day in practice. You can make this happen!"

Craig's center responded, "This is a whole team of Tonys."

"Shut up! This team has nothing on Tony," Craig said. "Now we're gonna go back out there, and I'm gonna toss it to James—deep. Let's go."

Craig's offense met the Spartans defense waiting at the ball, already in a crouching position.

"Blue 42, hike!" Craig yelled.

The ball came to him, and he stepped back. The offensive line moved back, but it did not allow the defense through. Craig saw James cutting across midfield without any defenders around him. He pulled the ball back and released it in James's direction.

Out of nowhere, a Spartans linebacker appeared. He saw the ball sailing over the action on the line of scrimmage and jumped into the air with a hand ready for an interception. He touched the ball with his middle finger, stopping the forward movement just enough to wrap the rest of his fingers around it. When he landed on the ground, the ball was back in the Spartans' control and 25 yards away from the Falcons end zone.

With a minute left in the quarter, the Spartans turned on the running game and managed to move the ball to the Falcons 6-yard line. They were threatening to score again.

CHAPTER ELEVEN

Tony Takes the Field

"O kay, Tony, you're in," Coach Johnson said. "Get out there and make some plays!"

Tony scanned the field as he separated his personal life from the game. His team was down. It might be his fault. This was his responsibility now. He went to the defensive huddle.

"We gotta stop them," said Phillip, the left defensive tackle.

"Relax," Tony said.

"Easy for you to say," Phillip retorted. "You've been sitting on the sideline all this time."

"Cut it, man," Travis said.

"Look, they have our backs against the wall," Tony said. "We've been in this position before, and we know how to get out of it. This is when we show them what we've got!"

The Spartans were already at the line of scrimmage at the 6-yard line to begin the second quarter. The Falcons defense approached their opponents at the ball. The center snapped the ball, and the linemen engaged.

This time, the holes were not there for the Spartans. Although the offensive line out-powered the Falcons, the defense stuffed the running lanes forcing the play to a standstill. The Spartans were able to gain one yard out of sheer force, but they had nowhere to go.

Back in the huddle, Tony complimented his team. "That's exactly what we need to do. They can't go anywhere without a hole. Stuff those things!"

The ball was at the 5-yard line, and the Spartans were prepared for the next play. The Falcons lined up and waited for the snap. They were so eager for the snap that Phillip jumped offsides. The penalty moved the Spartans even closer to the goal line.

"Come on," Travis railed.

"Relax, man, relax," Tony said. "This is gonna happen. We are turning things around, but mistakes are gonna happen. Phillip, you good?"

"Yeah, man," Phillip said.

"Good, then let's get back out there and stuff them," Tony said, looking into each of his teammates' eyes.

This time, the Falcons made it to the ball before the Spartans.

"Remember, this is goal-line defense!" Tony shouted.

Two and a half minutes had already passed in the second quarter. The Spartans center snapped the ball, and the front lines met like the upper and lower teeth of an alligator. A Spartan running back took the ball from the quarterback and saw the wall before him. There was no hole. At that moment, he decided to make a leap over the wall of linemen. He planted both feet into the turf and bent his knees. He pushed with all his might, making his legs straight again. His feet left the ground, and he soon found himself sailing over the linemen and into the end zone.

Out of nowhere, Tony appeared. He confronted the running back like a cat attacking its prey. The running back was instantly changing direction in midair. The ball carrier actually landed on his back in the same spot he had originally left the ground from.

The clock continued to tick as the fans cheered. Both sides untangled themselves and prepared for the field goal. Not much changed in personnel. Tony remained on the field, and the Spartans quarterback did, too.

Players on both teams lined up for the fourth-down play with eight minutes left in the quarter. The ball was snapped, but the quarterback did not hold the ball for the kicker. Instead, he stood up and looked for his receiver faking a block, moving into the end zone. The entire Falcons defense stampeded for the Spartans kicker and didn't see the Spartans receiver breaking free. The quarterback saw his target wide open and passed it to him in the end zone. The Spartans scored another touchdown.

Tony looked at the score. The Spartans were now up by thirteen points, and they were sure to make the extra point. He knew his defense was going to have to play much tougher to contend with the Spartans. They were even better than he had thought.

The Spartans made the extra point, and the Falcons kick return team went to the field. Lester ran by Tony during the shuffle.

"Remember what you've done in practice," Tony said.

Lester nodded and settled into his position in Falcons territory. The clock started again, and the ball was kicked into the Falcons end zone. The Falcons offense would start on the 20-yard line.

Craig brought the offense from the huddle to the line of scrimmage. He was determined to start moving the ball.

"Ready, set, hike!" Craig said.

The ball went to Craig, and he stepped back to place the ball in Lester's hands. The offensive line created a hole, and Lester was small enough to squeeze through it for 5 yards.

Back in the huddle, Craig called for a pass play. He remembered the interception he had thrown last time, and he had to remain patient.

"I'm going short this time," Craig said. "Front line, make sure you stay on the linebackers."

The huddles broke, and the lines converged on the Falcons 25-yard line. Craig called for the ball, and the play began. A missed block gave a defensive tackle a chance to sack Craig. He backpedaled a few yards and saw his target wide open. The ball spiraled out of his hand, and the receiver caught it. The receiver was tackled just seconds after the reception. However, the Falcons managed to gain 5 more yards, picking up a key first down.

"Okay, we are going to Lester," Craig said. "Make it happen, guy."

Craig waited for his players to line up by checking both sides of his line.

"Down, set, red 19, hike!" Craig yelled.

The ball went from the center to Craig to Lester in less than a second. Lester ran across the line of scrimmage just as the offensive line made contact. The Spartans defensive line did not even see Lester move. He approached a huge linebacker and spun around him. Another linebacker was not fast enough to catch Lester. He gained 22 yards when a Spartan cornerback finally hit him. The Falcons had moved the ball into Spartans territory with three minutes left in the quarter.

All the players returned to their huddles except for Lester. He remained on the ground, and he wasn't moving. A referee blew his whistle, and Coach Johnson jogged over to Lester with the team trainer. Lester did not make a sound, but he was blinking his eyes.

"You all right, son?" Coach Johnson asked.

Lester nodded, struggling to his feet. Tony ran to the field and helped him up.

"Come on, man," Tony said. "Walk it off. We need you, buddy."

Tony helped Lester to the sideline, and the ref started the game again. Craig brought the offense to the line and shot a mean look to the defensive cornerback, who had just knocked Lester out of the game.

"Down, set, hike!" Craig barked.

The ball went to the backup running back, but he had nowhere to run at the line of scrimmage. The Falcons did not gain any yards on first down.

"Line, you gotta make your blocks," Craig said. "We can't go anywhere if we cannot run. Let's go!"

Craig received the ball on the next snap and went back for a pass. The Spartans anticipated the pass and sent every lineman toward Craig. Two defensive linemen broke through the Falcons offensive line and darted toward Craig. He continued to move back; he could not see an opening. He was about to throw the ball out of bounds, but he had waited too long. Suddenly, two Spartan defenders hit him from both sides. The Falcons lost 7 yards and were back in their own territory for third down.

A little more than a minute remained in the half as both sides ran to their huddles.

"Just give me enough time to toss another short one," Craig said, trying to keep calm.

At the line, with the half coming to an end, Craig took the snap and looked for his receiver a few yards out. He was open again, and Craig connected. This time the receiver managed to shake a defender and move the ball toward the Spartans end zone. The same cornerback that had hit Lester managed to take down the Falcons receiver at the 26-yard line.

"Time out," Craig said to the ref. He ran to Coach Johnson. "Let's try for another first down."

"There isn't enough time," Coach Johnson said.

"Come on, coach," Craig said. "I do this all the time in practice."

"We need to get the points. Field goal team, on the field!" Coach Johnson shouted.

"Man!" Craig yelled.

"Get off the field," Coach Johnson said. "If you have a problem with my decision, you can stay out to think about it."

Both sides set up for the field goal try. Craig's replacement was skilled enough to hold the ball for the kicker, Frank Bellow. The ref blew the whistle to resume the game, and the center aimed for the holder. With the change in personnel, the Spartans thought the Falcons were going to fake the kick. The kicker took one last practice kick and walked backward from the holder to get in the correct position for a field goal.

"Hike," the holder called.

The ball went right to the holder, and the kicker ran toward the ball before it was settled. The kicker made contact with the ball, and it just barely sailed over the hands of the defense. The strong kick moved more like a kickoff. The eyes of every fan, player, and coach followed the ball. It continued spinning over the Spartans end zone and through the goal posts. The Falcons were on the scoreboard.

As the cheers died down, and the Falcons sent another kickoff to the Spartans, the first half came to a close. The Spartans took a knee to run down the clock, satisfied with their eleven-point lead over the Falcons.

CHAPTER TWELVE

Leading the Charge

Heavy breathing filled the concrete locker room. A few sore players stretched on the ground, but most were sitting on a bench drinking water and staring at the floor. Coach Johnson entered the room and paced.

"You don't need me to tell you what's going on out there," Coach Johnson said. "You guys are letting them scare you. They are all looks—can't play any better than you."

Tony looked up, irritated by the team's first-half performance. He looked to the leader, Craig, walking out of the bathroom. The leader needed a leader. Tony looked at Lester. Lester looked right back at Tony. Tony nodded to him. He knew that Lester was key to the second half of the game. And Lester thought the same of Tony.

"Like I said, you are all thinking too much; use your instincts," Coach Johnson said. "Take a few minutes, but no more, and let's get back out there."

Craig was the first to move toward the door to the field. Lester followed along with the rest of the team. Tony was the last player to stand. Coach Johnson leaned in front of Tony.

"Tony, I know you have things on your mind, and I know you don't want to talk about them," Coach Johnson said. "All you need to think about now is what you are going to do on that field. That's it."

The Spartans were practicing on the field when Tony joined his team for a quick lap. He looked to the bleachers. Shannon stood cheering, clapping her hands for the team. Ms. Parker sat alone with a stack of tests to correct. He knew those two would be there. He was really looking for his mother and brother. He hoped that they would find time to come to the game.

The Falcons could not run many practice plays before it was time for the second-half kickoff. The Spartans sent the ball right to Lester on the Falcons 15-yard line. Lester squinted his eyes as he tucked the ball under his arm. He saw a path his teammates were creating, and he followed. He began to see the dark uniforms of his opponents. Yards passed while individual battles continued between the teams' players. Lester did not stop his forward charge.

Finally, a wall of Spartans uniforms stopped Lester in his tracks. The fans' cheers echoed in his head as he tried to concentrate on the field. He could not make out the yard line. A few of his teammates helped him to the sideline.

"That was perfect, Lester," Tony said. "All the way to the 38-yard line. This is just the way we need to start the half."

Lester needed to take a seat. He was still recovering from the play.

"Can you get out there again, buddy?" Tony asked.

Craig was already running the first play as Lester nodded to Tony. Lester saw the coach motioning to him to be ready for the next play. He used his hands to keep himself steady on the bench. He struggled to reach his feet and had to sit back down.

"You sure you're okay?" Tony asked.

Lester did not respond.

"Coach, you gotta send someone else in for Lester," Tony said.

"Lester, you need to see the trainer?" Coach Johnson asked.

After hearing Coach Johnson's question, Lester immediately came to his feet and walked to the coach for the play. Craig was running a passing play on the team's second down.

"You have them run a tackle trap, okay?" said Coach Johnson to Lester.

Lester nodded and turned to run the play to Craig on the field. Tony grabbed Lester just before he left the sideline.

"You sure you're okay, man?" Tony asked. "You want to be able to walk off the field after the game."

"I can do this, Tony," Lester said, and he ran the play to Craig in the huddle.

As the Falcons offense lined up for the play, Lester rubbed his eyes, hoping to increase his concentration. The aftereffects of the last hit were still influencing him. He heard the play start with a snap of the ball into Craig's hands. Craig stepped back and saw the hole open for Lester.

Suddenly, Lester felt the leathery texture of the ball in his hands, and his body automatically took him to the hole in front of him. He was like a robot being controlled remotely. He had run this play so many times that his body ran the play without his mind. Regardless, the hole was there, and the only thing between him and the end zone was the same Spartans defender who brought him down during the kickoff.

Lester remembered the practices he had gone through and all the hard hits Tony had unleashed on him. He imagined his opponent was Tony. If he could contend with Tony—the best linebacker in the city—he could contend with any defender. Lester concentrated on the linebacker and turned his body into a living rocket.

The linebacker prepared to hit Lester, but Lester had already made his move. Lester nailed the Spartans linebacker so low that he knocked the linebacker off balance. Instead of going down with the would-be tackler, Lester ran right over him and didn't stop until he made it all the way to the end zone.

Lester was dizzy from all that had happened, but he could hear the crowd roaring.

"Yeah, man!" Tony cheered.

The Falcons were down by five points, and they still had a quarter and a half to make their comeback. The team slapped Lester on the head to celebrate his touchdown. The extra point was successful for the Falcons, and the special teams ran to the field for the kickoff.

After the kickoff, Tony took his defense to the field for a huddle. He thought about Lester's effort. He saw the Spartans offense huddling across from his defense, and he was determined to stop any forward movement from his opponents.

The Spartans went straight into more running plays, and the clock ticked down. The Spartans used every down and slowly moved the ball downfield. Like the first set of plays in the first quarter, they were able to move the ball 3 or 4 yards every down. They passed the 50-yard line and made it into Falcons territory.

Frustration washed through Tony's mind. He participated in almost every tackle, but the Spartans were too strong. They were able to move the Falcons defense with pure strength. He knew he had to get to the quarterback if he wanted to stop them from scoring another touchdown.

The center snapped the ball to the Spartans quarterback. Tony moved before any other player and slipped by the offensive line. He raced into the backfield with his eyes on the quarterback. Luckily for Tony, the quarterback also moved back for a rare passing play. Nothing could stop Tony now. His shoulder pad cracked against the quarterback's chest. Locked like rams on a mountain, Tony pushed his opponent back for a sack.

"Let's keep this up!" Tony admonished his defense.

The raucous crowd was jubilant as the teams lined up for the next play. The field seemed to quake with their cheers. Tony went to his ready position, determined to make the same play. The Spartans quarterback looked around.

"Down, set, red 42, hike!" said the Spartans quarterback, but the center did not snap the ball. It was a fake—a hard count to fool the defense.

Tony moved into the offensive line while everyone else remained still. The ref blew his whistle.

"Offsides, defense!" yelled the ref.

As a consequence of the penalty, the ball moved 5 yards closer to the Spartans goal. Tony tried to swallow, but his mouth was too dry. At this time, only a few minutes remained in the quarter, and, again, the Spartans were making the Falcons look foolish. He shook his head and moved to the huddle.

Tony knew he could not lose confidence. Everyone makes mistakes. His team needed his leadership, and a leader keeps going, even in hard times.

After assuring his team that they could stop these guys, Tony regrouped his defense and approached the line again. The Spartans went back to the running game and started moving the ball again—yard by yard.

As the quarter came to an end, the Spartans made one more attempt to move the ball forward. As the ball was snapped, Tony saw the Spartans running back squirming through a hole, and he engaged him. Tony hit the runner so hard that the ball came loose and bounced on the grass.

"Fumble!" Tony yelled.

Both teams slowly realized what had happened. Players from both teams jumped to the ground, hoping to snag the loose ball. The shape of the ball made recovery difficult. Eventually, a heap of players formed over the ball. The ref blew his whistle to see who had gained possession.

The referee moved Spartans and Falcons players out of the way so he could determine who had the ball. A Falcons player was curled around a Spartan, and they both struggled for a moment. The referee stood up and pointed toward the Spartans goal. The quarter was over, and, though the Spartans still had the ball, Tony was finally getting to them.

CHAPTER THIRTEEN

The Fourth Quarter

The teams switched sides for the final quarter of the game. The Spartans still possessed the ball. Tony knew that the Falcons couldn't allow another Spartans touchdown. Their ability to eat time off the clock could make an extra touchdown the end of the game.

Tony huddled the Falcons defense. His teammates were weary eyed with fatigue and nervousness. Even Travis seemed a little uneasy.

"Listen," Tony said. "We stopped these guys, and they know it. In fact, they know we are on to their running game. These guys don't run the ball just because they can't pass. They want to run down the clock. They want to get out of here. They don't want to play. They are afraid to play. You guys are here to play the game, and we are about to make it ours!"

"Yeah!" Travis shouted in agreement.

"Let's do this," Tony said.

With Tony's words, the Falcons defense lost all fear and approached the Spartans at the Falcons 31-yard line. Tony went into his ready position and nodded to Travis, who nodded back with his characteristic grin. The fans cheered in anticipation as the Spartans quarterback called for the ball. The snap sent Travis hurtling toward the backfield in search of the runner. The running back was so shocked to see Travis that he ran right into Tony. The Spartans lost a yard in a game where every yard was as valuable as gold.

"That's right," Tony said, after delivering a perfect tackle.

"Keep them coming," Travis said to Tony. "But watch out. They may start passing the ball if we don't let them run anywhere."

Sure enough, the loss of yards forced the Spartans to throw a pass to regain the yards they had lost. The pass was short, and the Falcons brought down the receiver. But the Spartans only had a few yards to go for a first down.

The Falcons came to the ball on third down, and Tony recognized the running formation.

"They're running it! They're running it!" Tony warned his teammates.

The Falcons reconfigured their formation for the run and waited for the snap. The quarterback received the ball, but he faked a handoff, fooling the Falcons defense. One Spartans receiver was open behind Tony. The Spartans quarterback tossed the ball right to his man. Luckily, Tony was able to spin around when the ball flew over his head, and he tackled the receiver.

The refs had to bring in the markers to see if the Spartans had achieved a first down. The fans chattered uncomfortably, and the players gathered around the ball.

"First down!" cried the ref.

"Dang!" Travis shouted. "They faked us out."

"Don't worry," Tony said.

"Don't worry?" Travis said, still shouting. "They are knocking on our door!"

"Travis!" Coach Johnson yelled from the sideline. "Direct that energy in a different way."

Twenty yards away from their end zone, the Spartans approached the ball with a four-point lead. The clock was spinning toward zero, and the Spartans continued to run the ball.

At the next snap, Travis charged toward the line of scrimmage and leaped over the combatants. He was in the backfield when he saw the handoff. While redirecting himself, he lost traction and twisted to the ground. He yelled in pain as Tony brought down the running back.

"Not now, man," Travis squirmed in pain, clutching his ankle. "Not now."

Travis rocked back and forth as Tony and the team trainer ran to him.

"Back off," Travis said. "No way you're taking me off the field."

Travis limped to the huddle.

"Man, don't push it," Phillip said.

"I got this," Travis said. "What's the plan?"

Tony saw the Falcons backup linebacker running toward the huddle.

"Travis," Coach Johnson yelled. "Get out of there!"

"What?" Travis yelled.

"Travis," Tony said. "Do what the man says."

"No way!" Travis said. "This is our game."

"Travis," Tony said, looking into his eyes. "You can't play. Look, you are leaning on Phillip. You can't make it *our* game with a busted ankle."

Travis's replacement entered the huddle. Tony looked at the replacement and then to Travis.

"We would not be in a position to win this game without you. But now you have to help us by getting off the field," Tony said.

Travis turned from the huddle, pushed Phillip aside, and limped to the sideline.

"He'll be okay," Tony said.

At this point, the fourth quarter was almost halfway over. A few yards every down pushed the Spartans closer and closer to the goal line. Clouds of steam formed over the helmets of all the running backs utilized by the Spartans offense. Tony made his tackles, but the Spartans made a little more progress with Travis on the sideline.

With two and a half minutes to go in the game, the Spartans were only 5 yards away from the end zone on third down. The fans in the bleachers were all standing to see the conclusion of this never-ending offensive run. The Falcons came to the line of scrimmage with a goal-line defense.

"Stop them!" Travis yelled.

Lester stood next to Travis and nodded. Shannon gripped her hands near her mouth, caught in the moment's tension. Even Ms. Parker had stopped correcting papers.

Tony looked at the Spartans ahead of him. The Spartans offensive formation was a little odd. He could usually predict the play by looking at the offensive formation, but this time it was unclear. The Spartans could pass, or they could run. Tony had told his teammates to expect a rush, but he wasn't so sure anymore. He did not want to change the plan at the last minute because he didn't want to cause confusion.

"Down, set, red 19, hike," roared the Spartans quarterback.

Tony had seen this play earlier in the quarter. The quarterback faked the handoff and went back to pass. The Falcons defense converged in the middle, expecting a rush. This time, Tony back-pedaled to the open receiver running across the Falcons end zone.

The ball left the quarterback's hand and flew like a hawk toward the receiver. The receiver's hands were ready, and his eyes followed the ball. Suddenly, Tony's body blinded him. Tony had jumped in front of him, hands ready for the catch. The receiver and the quarterback realized what was happening and could only stand and watch. Tony intercepted the football.

With most of the players on both teams smashed in one spot on the field, Tony saw his team's goal posts in the other end zone. He planted one foot in the ground and used it to gain the momentum he needed to sprint to the other end of the field. The quarterback was still in shock as Tony raced by him. A few smaller running backs chased after Tony, but he was too big for them to tackle him.

Tony only saw bright lights and a goal post as the yards passed by. He could not stop himself from blinking. When he opened his eyes, he saw the people in his life. His legs continued to move forward, but he saw Craig, Lester, and Travis without helmets. He saw Coach Johnson and his math teacher smiling at him. He remembered Shannon's face, her kiss, and the help she had given him. His brother was at his side. But this time, his brother was his age, and they were both playing football. Finally, he saw his mom and, behind her, his father. His father placed his arm around Jasmine just as they disappeared.

Tony was in the end zone. With just under a minute left, the Falcons had the lead, 17–14. The score did not change again. Tony heard the Falcons fans cheering, and he knew his teammates were hugging him. He wanted to enjoy this moment. He knew soon enough he would have much more important responsibilities to worry about.

CHAPTER FOURTEEN

Tony's Choice

Tony smiled at his teammates as they celebrated in the locker room. He sat on an empty bench with his helmet in his lap and Lester on his left. Lester still wore his helmet.

"Why are you still wearing your helmet?" Tony asked.

Lester unbuckled his chinstrap and took off his helmet. His long hair tumbled about and settled on his shoulders. He turned to Tony.

"Thanks for being there, Tony," Lester said. "You've always had my back."

Tony showed his white teeth through his smile and laughed. He came to his feet and rubbed

Lester's head. Craig slammed the palms of his hands into Tony's shoulder pads.

"You're just too bad, man," said Craig with a raised cheek.

"You're pretty bad yourself," Tony replied.

Travis walked over. "You guys should go on a honeymoon," Travis teased.

They all laughed until they saw Coach Johnson approaching. Coach Johnson never celebrated in the open. He wasn't angry, but he wasn't smiling either. He nodded at the players and headed into his office.

As Tony sat on the bench enjoying the victory, he thought about his father. He remembered the job he had to find to support his mother and brother. He remembered Shannon and the things he had to learn in school. His reorganized his responsibilities and priorities in his head.

Despite the victory and his love of the game, football was the least of his concerns. His team would understand because they had learned a lot from him. The game of life suddenly became much more important than football.

Tony was not afraid as he entered Coach Johnson's office. Tony's eyes did not look away from his coach, and he did not wait for Coach Johnson to talk first. He knew what he had to say, and he only wanted respect in return.

"Coach, I've got to quit."

Slowly, the coach sat up straighter. He tilted his head and wrinkled his forehead as he stared at Tony. "What are you talking about? Did something happen out there that I don't know about? Were you injured?"

"Some things have happened, but not on the field. I love football. I love being part of this team; I love the practices and the games," Tony said.

"Then I don't get it. Why are you quitting?" Coach Johnson asked.

Tony hesitated. He didn't want to complain about his problems. They were his to solve. But he had to show his coach that he was serious.

"My family needs me. My mother lost one of her jobs, and she needs me to bring in some money until she can find another. And there's my brother, Tyson. He needs someone around right now to keep him out of trouble. And then there's school.

I'm nearly failing math. I can't do all this and still play football."

"But football could be your future. You are good enough to get a college scholarship. It could be your ticket to a better life, and you just want to dump it?" Coach Johnson said, shaking his head.

"I don't want to . . . I have to. My family and my education are my future," said Tony as he moved toward the door. "I'll clean my stuff out of my locker."

"Wait! Hold on for just a second. You got to promise me something, okay? Do what you have to do to help your family. Focus on your classes. But don't forget about football. Promise me that when you get your life back on track . . . and I know that you will because I know how hard you will work at it . . . you will come back. That door is always open, your locker stays the same, and there will always be a place for you on my team. Promise me." Coach Johnson put his hand out for Tony to shake.

Tony's eyes looked at the coach and then at his hand. He slowly reached out with a smile, shook the coach's hand, and said, "I promise."

Read other titles in the series **A CHAMPION SPORTS STORY**

BATTING NINTH

Chad is a terrible hitter. But when a new coach arrives, things start to change. This exciting story will keep you flipping the pages as the Rangers strive for the championship trophy, and Chad learns the value of playing the game the right way.

Library Ed. ISBN 978-0-7660-3886-8
Paperback ISBN 978-1-4644-0001-8

MATTY IN THE GOAL

Matty loves soccer, but he isn't any good at it. When he volunteers to be his team's new goalie, he hopes to become an important part of the team. Follow Matty in this kickin' soccer story as he tries to go from benchwarmer to goalie superstar.

Library Ed. ISBN 978-0-7660-3877-6
Paperback ISBN 978-1-4644-0003-2

ROUNDING THIRD, HEADING HOME!

Can Jacob's Little League team, Morey's Funeral Home, really go from worst to first? You won't be able to put down this funny, action-packed story about a ragtag team going for glory when they meet their nemesis for a shot at the championship.

Library Ed. ISBN 978-0-7660-3876-9
Paperback ISBN 978-1-4644-0002-5

TODD GOES FOR THE GOAL

Todd is a great soccer player, but he hates how the bullies on his team, Highfield High, cheat to win games. When his family moves to a new town, Todd must confront these bullies on the field. Can Todd carry his new team to victory?

Library Ed. ISBN 978-0-7660-3887-5
Paperback ISBN 978-1-4644-0000-1